Rosie's Double Dare

Rosie

Lizzie

Bill

Rosie's Double Dare

by Robie H. Harris

illustrated by Tony DeLuna

Helen George Peter Norman

Alfred A. Knopf • New York

J
H

Other Knopf Capers books

Man from the Sky by Avi
Running Out of Time by Elizabeth Levy
The Case of the Weird Street Firebug by Carol Russell Law
The Mystery on Bleeker Street by William H. Hooks
The Robot and Rebecca by Jane Yolen

This is a Borzoi Book
Published by Alfred A. Knopf, Inc.

Copyright © 1980 by Robie H. Harris
Illustrations Copyright © 1980 by Alfred A. Knopf, Inc.
All rights reserved under International and Pan-American
Copyright Conventions. Published in the United States by
Alfred A. Knopf, Inc., New York, and simultaneously in
Canada by Random House of Canada Limited, Toronto.
Distributed by Random House, Inc., New York.
Manufactured in the United States of America.
10 9 8 7 6 5 4 3 2 1

Library of Congress Cataloging in Publication Data
Harris, Robie H   Rosie's double dare (Capers)
Summary: When she accepts two dares from the
Willard Street Gang in order to play baseball
with them, eight-year-old Rosie finds
herself on television on the field of a Red Sox
baseball game. [1. Gangs—Fiction.
2. Baseball—Fiction] I. Title.
PZ7.H2436Ro [Fic] 79–26907
ISBN 0–394–84459–9 pbk.
ISBN 0–394–94459–3 lib. bdg.

To the Meadows Road Gang

Contents

Rosie's Double Dare

1 · Shrimp Rules

"Hey, George! Do you know the joke about the jump rope?" asked Rosie.

George was reading the new baseball yearbook. He didn't answer.

Rosie straightened her glasses, leaned over, and tickled her brother George on the end of his nose. George pushed away her hand.

"George Davidson, answer me," whined Rosie.

"No," said George, still looking at his book. "I don't know the joke about the jump rope."

"Oh, *skip it!*" Rosie laughed.

"That joke stinks," George groaned. He started reading again.

"Wanna hear the one about the skunk, then?" she giggled.

"Keep quiet, Rosie," said George.

"This will be the last joke," she said. "I promise."

"I told you, no more dumb jokes," George warned, holding his fist in front of her face. "You'd better move, Rosie."

Rosie ran down the steps of the front stoop, across Willard Street, and into the park in front of their house. George dropped his book and ran after her.

"Don't you want to hear the one about the skunk?" Rosie yelled, running hard.

George screamed, "I told you NO!"

"Forget it, it *stinks!*" shrieked Rosie back at George.

"Just like you!" he shouted.

As George was about to tackle Rosie, Mrs. Samuels and her dog, Elmer, crossed in front of him. George tripped over Elmer and slid onto the grass.

"Children! children!" cried Mrs. Samuels, swinging her cane in the air. Mrs. Samuels was seventy-three years old and lived in a house across the park from Rosie and George.

"Sorry, Mrs. Samuels," muttered George. "Sorry. . . ."

Just then, George's friends, "the Willard Street Gang," ran into the park. George jumped up and ran over to them, shaking his head. It was Mrs. Samuels who had named George's friends "The Willard Street Gang".

"Your baby sister getting to you again?" asked Bill as he tossed a softball in the air.

"I am *not* his baby sister," said Rosie. "I am his younger sister. I am almost nine years old—only two and a half years younger than George."

"We know how old you are, Rosie," said Bill. "Cool your jets. Hey George, wanna play some baseball?"

"All right! Anything to get away from this shrimp," said George, pointing at his sister.

"I'm not a shrimp," said Rosie as she

jumped up on the park bench next to Mrs. Samuels. "See, I'm the tallest of all. So how could I be a shrimp, huh, huh . . .?"

Rosie always said "huh, huh" when she was a little bit mad, not really mad, but just mad enough to still want George to listen to her. She knew that George never listened to her when she was really mad . . . when she was screaming. George called her a maniac when she was screaming and ranting and raving. Rosie knew she wasn't a real maniac—that was just George's way of insulting her. Sometimes, Rosie said "huh, huh" when she was scared, too. Saying "huh, huh" helped her from showing that she was really mad or really scared.

George ignored Rosie and turned to the gang. He counted up the kids—Lizzie, Bill, Helen, Peter.

"We only have five players, counting me," said George. "Where's Norman?"

"Norman hurt his foot. He has to stay off it—for today anyway," said Helen.

"We can't play with uneven teams. It

won't be fair," said George, who was always the captain when the gang played baseball.

"I'll play," Rosie said.

"You'll play?" asked George. "How can you play? You don't even know the rules. Besides, you're too shrimpy. You can't even bat."

"I do too know the rules. I've been watching the gang play for two years. Give me a chance," said Rosie.

"Yeah," Lizzie said. "Give her a chance."

"Oh, all right," said George. "One chance. You can play three innings. If you can hit, you can play. If you can't hit, you can't play."

The first time Rosie got up to bat, she straightened her glasses, choked up on the bat, and bent her knees. She placed her feet so far apart it seemed that if a gust of wind blew, it might push her over flat on her face. Then she bent forward at the waist and stuck her fanny way out in back.

"Why are you standing like that?" asked Peter.

8

"I saw somebody bat like this on TV. If it's good enough for TV, it's good enough for me," said Rosie, clutching the bat. It took just three pitches for Rosie to strike out.

Each time Rosie got up to bat, she would stick her fanny way out in back. And each time Rosie got up to bat, she would strike out. George kept reminding her, "This isn't TV, you know."

When Rosie came up to bat in the third inning, the first pitch sailed a good two feet over her head. But Rosie swung with all her might, spun around, fell over backwards, and landed on her fanny.

"Did I hit it?" she yelled, searching around for her glasses.

"No, you missed again," said George. He shook his head in disgust. "You'd better leave the game. You're no good."

Rosie started to cry. "I'm doing my best. I'm doing my best."

"But you can't even hit the ball," said George.

Rosie wiped her eyes. She thought for a minute. "I've got it," she said. "If you guys could roll the ball on the ground, I could hit it. I could do it. Why can't you guys pitch me grounders, like Dad pitches me grounders? You know I can hit grounders, so, huh, huh. . . ."

"Rosie," said George, "grounders aren't in this game. Grounders aren't part of the rules. We have to follow the rules."

"I want grounders!" Rosie shouted.

George put his hands over his ears. "Boy," he said. "For a shrimp, you sure make a lot of noise."

"I'm not a shrimp. I'm not a shrimp." Rosie's voice was getting louder and louder. Soon she was screaming, "I am not a shrimp! I am not a shrimp!"

Suddenly Rosie stopped screaming, put on her glasses, and looked over at George. "I dare you to let me have grounders," she said, pointing her finger at George.

"I can't let you have grounders. They aren't in the rules. We'd have to change the rules and make special rules for a shrimp. Shrimp rules," said George.

"I dare you to let me have shrimp rules," said Rosie. Her voice was quiet, but sure.

George thought for a minute. "I double dare you," said George. "I double dare you to do something to prove to the gang that you are not a shrimp. In fact, I double dare you to do a dare that the gang tells you to do. And if you do the dare the exact way the gang tells you to do it, you can play with us. You can have your stupid shrimp rules."

"It's a deal," said Rosie nervously.

"Is that okay with all of you?" asked George, looking at the gang. They all nodded yes.

"But what's the dare, huh, huh? What's the dare?" asked Rosie.

"The gang will decide and tell you after dinner," said George with a big smile. "Is it a deal? Rosie?" he asked, holding out his hand. "Deal?"

"Deal," said Rosie as she shook hands with George.

Rosie wasn't smiling as she walked up the steps to her front door. She turned around and looked back at the park. She could see George and the gang huddled in a circle.

2 · Soggy Spaghetti

Rosie looked out her living room window. She could still see the gang huddled together in the park.

"I wonder what they're going to make me do," she thought. "They won't make me do anything too awful, too scary, I'm sure they won't. . . . But what if they do? What if they make me hide in the basement until after it's dark or take my clothes off and do a handstand in the middle of the park, or call up my teacher and tell him I love him?"

Rosie turned away from the window and curled up on the couch. She twirled the ends of her hair around her fingers. It had taken her one whole year to grow it down to her shoulders. Rosie loved long hair, even though it always hung over her eyes and got in her food. She was always getting egg or cereal in her hair. One day, when she got maple syrup on the ends of her hair, her mother had threatened to cut it all off and give her a crew cut. Since then Rosie had worn her hair back in a ponytail.

Suddenly, Rosie stopped twisting her hair. She sat upright. "Maybe they'll make me cut off all my hair, for the dare. My hair for the dare!" She almost cried out loud. Rosie had once seen a picture in the newspaper of a big kid who had made his little sister cut off her hair. "So it could happen. It could happen to me," she thought.

Just then, the front door slammed and George ran into the living room. He was grinning.

"Sure you still want to do it?" he asked Rosie. "The gang's ready for you."

"Tell me what the dare is," said Rosie,

stamping her foot hard on the living room floor.

"Dinner!" Mr. Davidson called. "The spaghetti's ready. Come and get it!"

As soon as Rosie and George sat down at the dining room table, their father served a bowl of spaghetti to George. Rosie pointed her finger at George and yelled, "Not fair! Not fair!"

"What's not fair?" asked Mr. Davidson.

"It's not fair that George got spaghetti before I did. He got served first. I'm gonna get served last. I hate being served last, huh, huh. I always get served last. I hate it!"

George put down his baseball fact book and looked straight at Rosie. "All you ever do, Rosie, is complain that everything's not fair. But I guess that's what shrimps do all the time—yell, fuss, and scream."

"George and Rosie, stop it!" Mrs. Davidson shouted.

"I don't yell, fuss, and scream!" screamed Rosie.

"Wanna bet?" laughed George.

"Yeah!" screamed Rosie in a louder voice.

"Well, that's just what you're doing now," said George, laughing hard.

Rosie was really mad. She swung her arms around in circles and bumped over the milk pitcher. The milk spilled so fast that George didn't have time to move away from the table. First it spilled into George's bowl of spaghetti. Then it dribbled all over George's baseball fact book and down onto his lap. George jumped backwards and knocked over his chair.

"You jerk, Rose Anne Davidson! You wrecked my book. My spaghetti's soggy. My clothes are soaked. And that's not fair, either, right? Huh, huh to you," said George.

Just as George began wiping the milk off his book, the doorbell rang.

"George, answer the door," said Mr. Davidson.

"I can't," said George, angrily. "My pants are wet. It's probably the gang. I don't want them to think I wet my pants."

Rosie giggled.

"Rosie, you answer the door," George said. "Tell the gang I'll be out in five minutes." A slight grin started to form on his lips.

Rosie walked to the door as slowly as possible. The door bell rang again, this time longer and louder. She opened the door and there stood Mr. Quirk, the downstairs tenant.

Mr. Quirk was always saying that George and Rosie were making noise when they were not doing a thing. Sometimes he complained when they were not even home. Just last week, he had called about the children running around the living room floor like a herd of elephants. But George

and Rosie hadn't even been home. Mr.
Davidson said Mr. Quirk was just a harmless
crank. But George, Rosie, and the gang
secretly wondered about him.

When Mr. Quirk talked, he pulled his lips
down over his teeth. Sometimes Rosie and
George thought his teeth looked pointy like
daggers. But other times, his teeth seemed
bigger and flatter. George said he bet Mr.
Quirk had lots of different sets of teeth—just
to make him look meaner.

As Rosie opened the door, Mr. Quirk walked right past her, through the front hall, and into the dining room. "Ah ha," he said, pointing at Rosie and George. "The children are home this time. You can't fool me," he went on. "Your children are making all the racket this time. Can't a man work in peace? This is the last time. . . ." Mr. Quirk stopped for a minute to grind his teeth. The sound made Rosie shiver. "If there's any more noise from the children, I will have to move out." Then he turned and left, slamming the door behind him.

"Rosie and George, you will have to cut out all this fighting," warned Mr. Davidson. "We cannot afford to lose our tenant. You two will just have to quiet down."

"Can't I go now?" asked George, getting up from the table. "I've got to change and meet the gang."

Rosie brushed her hands over her hair. Suddenly she was sure the gang was going to dare her to cut her hair. "Maybe I should have short hair again," she said to her parents.

"I like your long hair," said her father.

"I could wear a wig," said Rosie a bit sadly.

"Like Mr. Quirk?" laughed her father.

"Does Mr. Quirk wear a wig?" Rosie asked.

"Oh, I don't know if he wears a wig or not. But his hair is always parted in the middle and it always lays so flat on his head. Tonight when he was upset, his hair didn't move an inch. I was just thinking he must wear a wig," answered her father.

"Well, I don't want to look like Mr. Quirk. I don't even ever want to see Mr. Quirk again," said Rosie. "He gives me the creeps."

Mr. Davidson hugged Rosie and said, "You could never look like Mr. Quirk, even with a wig."

Rosie heard the gang calling, "Rosie, Rosie." She ran over and gave her mother a very big hug. Then she walked out the door and over to the park.

3 · The Dare

The gang was back in a huddle. Rosie stopped when she got to the edge of the park and looked back toward the house. Her father was standing at the front door. Rosie felt like running back to him and calling this whole dare business off. "So what if I'm a shrimp," she thought. Rosie looked back at her father. Then she looked over at the gang. "But I do want my shrimp rules," she thought again.

Rosie walked over to the gang. Lizzie reached out her hand and said, "Here, Rosie. Sit in the middle of the gang. George will read the rules of the dare. If you agree to them, the dare is on. And if you do the dare, you can have your shrimp rules."

Rosie's knees were shaking. She held them tight and looked down at the ground. She could feel the *huh, huh's* racing all over her body, getting louder and louder. They were getting so loud that she didn't even know if she would be able to hear George's voice. But when her brother read the first rule, the *huh, huh's* stopped and she knew the dare had really begun.

George took a tiny pad out of his pocket, flipped over the cover, and began to read in a loud clear voice:

"Rule number one. The only people to know about the dare are all Willard Street Gang members and Rose Ann Davidson. If Rosie tells anyone about the dare, or talks to anyone about it, even after she has done it, the shrimp rules are off.

"Rule number two. You must do the dare exactly as we tell it to you. If you change it in any way, the shrimp rules are off.

"Rule number three. If you complete the dare, the shrimp rules are on.

"If you agree to all the rules, then shake hands with every member of the gang. When you have completed the dare we will teach you the secret Willard Street Gang handshake."

Rosie stood up and tried to act brave as she shook each gang member's hand. But she could feel the sweat on her palm as she shook George's hand. George wasn't grinning anymore. In fact, he looked worried.

Rosie sat down again. She hung onto her ponytail while George began to read off the dare. "This won't be so bad," she thought. "I guess it'll be worth a haircut to play with the gang and learn their secret handshake." Rosie had been trying to find out the secret handshake for over a year now. She began to breathe easier.

"Stand up, Rosie," said George. Rosie wondered whether her brother was going to be the one to cut off her hair. She stood up and George started reading.

"Rosie Davidson, on the day of June nineteenth, sometime during the day of Saturday, June nineteenth . . ."

"That's tomorrow," Lizzie whispered to Rosie.

". . . you will," George went on and looked Rosie straight in the eye. Rosie could hear his voice shake. "You will sneak into Mr. Quirk's apartment, find at least one set of his false teeth, more if possible, and bring them to us in the park. Then you will return them to wherever you found them without anyone, except for the Willard Street Gang, ever, ever knowing that you've done this dare."

Rosie didn't say anything.

"Do you understand?" asked George.

Rosie couldn't say anything.

"You have to do it before six tomorrow evening and then you'll get your shrimp rules," George said.

"It'll be okay, Rosie," said Lizzie. "Mr. Quirk goes out every afternoon between noon and one o'clock to have lunch at the Morales Coffee Shop. The gang has been watching him and following him for days. We really want to find out a lot about his teeth—how many sets he has. I'll bet he has a pair of fangs like Dracula. . . . Anyway, you can be the one to prove he has lots of sets of false teeth."

"And then you can play baseball with the gang," said Helen. "We could use another girl. And you're a good runner."

"But how will I get into his apartment?" asked Rosie, trying to hold back her tears. She wondered what he did with so many different sets of false teeth.

"The gang's checked out his place, too.

We know almost everything about him—except for the teeth," said Peter. "In the hot weather, he always leaves his back window open. You're small enough to get in."

"You can do it, Rosie," said George.

Rosie stood up and turned her back on George. "Oh, shut up, George," she said. Then she raced across the park, up the steps, into the house, and into her room. She threw herself on her bed.

Mrs. Davidson followed Rosie upstairs. "What's wrong?" she asked, sitting down on the bed. "Did you hurt yourself?"

Rosie shook her head no. "But I've changed my mind about my hair. I don't want you to cut it off, not one single strand."

"I won't cut your hair, Rosie, if you don't want me to. But tell me what's wrong. Your face is all flushed." Rosie's face felt hot. "Did George do something to you?" Rosie wanted to tell her mother yes, tell her all about the dare. Then maybe the dare would go away and things could be just like they'd been before.

"Daddy thought maybe you weren't feeling well at dinner," said her mother in a soft voice.

"Yes, that's it," Rosie said. "That's it. I have a headache."

"You played outside all day. It must be the heat. What were you and the gang talking about out there, anyway?" her mother asked.

"Oh, they were . . . they were just going over the rules, the rules of baseball, so I could play better. They were really being nice to me. I'm getting so good that they may let me play in all their games," said Rosie.

"That's great, Rosie," Mrs. Davidson said. "Why don't I read you a story now? Then you can go to bed early and get a good night's sleep. I'm sure that will make your headache go away."

Her mother read her a story and kissed her good night. But Rosie still had trouble falling asleep. She tried to count the hours until noon the next day, the time she would

27

be entering Mr. Quirk's basement apartment. The last time Rosie had been there was with her mother. It was the week before Mr. Quirk had moved in. She tried to remember what the apartment looked like. But all she could remember was that it was very dark—that there were hardly any windows.

Just as she was about to fall asleep, Rosie heard George's footsteps on the stairs. She felt wide awake again. "And what if I get caught by Mr. Quirk?" she thought. "What would he do to me?" She started to sweat and then told herself that she wasn't really scared. It was the heat that was keeping her up.

Rosie tossed and turned all night.

4 · Chattering Teeth

The next morning, right after breakfast, Rosie decided she needed a disguise. She went into the big hall closet and closed the door behind her. She looked around and found an old rain jacket and a pair of mittens. "I'll need these so I won't leave fingerprints." Then she found her father's old fishing hat. It had a big brim and flaps that ran from one ear all the way down around the back of the neck and over to the other ear. "This will hide my hair so no one will know it's me." Then she grabbed a pair of sunglasses to complete her disguise. Rosie stuffed all these things into a shopping

29

bag and rushed out to the park. The gang looked up when they saw her coming.

"I've got all my stuff," Rosie yelled.

"Shush," said Peter and pointed to Mrs. Samuels, who was sitting on the bench with Elmer.

"I came here to show you my disguise," said Rosie in a low voice.

"A disguise?" asked George. "Why do you need a disguise?"

"Good detectives always wear disguises. I don't want to be recognized. That's that. Want to see?" she asked. "It's all in this bag."

"Leave it in there," said Lizzie. "You can change in the bushes—when it's time."

"Okay," said Rosie. "But all of you better stay here, right here, so when I get the teeth I can show them to you." Everyone nodded yes.

Rosie's knees started to shake.

"What's wrong, Rosie?" asked Lizzie.

"I'm worried I'll have to go to jail—for breaking and entering," said Rosie. "I've seen that happen on TV. I don't want to go to jail."

"Don't be silly," said George. "We wouldn't make you do something that you'd go to jail for. Besides, Mr. Quirk lives in our house. You can't go to jail for breaking and entering your own house."

"You're sure?" asked Rosie.

"I'm sure," said George.

George looked over at Mrs. Samuels. "Hey, what about her?" he asked, looking worried.

"I'll take care of her. She likes me," said Norman, who was back playing ball with the gang. But he still limped a little because of his hurt foot.

"Hey, look," said Lizzie in a hushed voice. "There goes Mr. Quirk. He's wearing an old rain hat . . . and it's not even raining. He is a weirdo."

"Who?" asked Rosie.

"Mr. Quirk, you dodo," said George. "You'd better do it now."

"Now?" said Rosie. "It's not noon yet."

"Rosie," said George, "he left early today—so go now!"

As quickly as he could, Norman walked over to Mrs. Samuels and began talking to her. He patted her dog, Elmer. Peter promised to keep a lookout for Mr. Quirk and delay him . . . somehow . . . if he came back early.

Rosie picked up her shopping bag and ran into the bushes. First she put on the rain jacket. Then the hat and the sunglasses. Finally she slipped on the mittens. "So I won't leave any fingerprints," said Rosie out loud. Then she picked up her flashlight. She tiptoed out of the bushes and over to the gang.

"Oh, no," moaned George. "This is not a circus, Rosie. You look like a clown."

"I don't look like a clown, George," answered Rosie. "I just look like a different person."

"You do look different," said George. "That's for sure."

"You look great, Rosie," said Lizzie. "I

would never have recognized you. Never!
Now you'd better get going."

Rosie raced to the back of Mr. Quirk's
apartment. She climbed right in the back
window. "This is pretty easy," she thought,
as she slipped over the windowsill and down
onto the floor. But then something moved.
Rosie froze in place. She saw two eyes
looking at her. She quickly turned on the

flashlight and shined it into the thing's eyes. The thing jumped and ran out of the room. Rosie tried to remember if Mr. Quirk had a cat, but she was so scared now that she couldn't think straight.

"Calm, down, Rosie," she said to herself. "All you have to do is get the teeth." She looked at her mittens. They were shaking. "Shaking mittens," she thought. "Quit shaking and start thinking. Where would the old crab keep his teeth?"

Rosie looked around the room again. "I wish it weren't so dark. Only creepy people live in dark places," she mumbled to herself.

Just then, Rosie heard a bell ringing. "Oh, no," she thought, "I've set off his burglar alarm. Now I *will* get arrested for breaking and entering. The creep had this trap set just for me. Oh, I wish George were here to explain to the police, huh, huh."

Rosie started to cry. Then she looked over at a table in the corner. Sitting on the table was a telephone. It rang and rang and then stopped ringing. Rosie wiped the sweat from her face. "How could I think *that* was a burglar alarm?" she said out loud.

Rosie walked into a narrow hall. Slowly, she opened the first door she saw. She looked into Mr. Quirk's bedroom and shined her flashlight around the room. It was full of books, not false teeth.

She opened another door. It was a closet, and heavy things fell out. More books. Rosie pushed them all back inside. Then she opened another door, the bathroom door.

Rosie looked around. No false teeth anywhere. She opened the medicine cabinet,

careful to do it with her mittens. She knew that time was running out, that Mr. Quirk might return at any minute.

Rosie's teeth began to chatter. She felt as if *she* had false teeth. She also felt as if someone was watching her. Slowly, she turned her head and looked at the shelf next to the medicine cabinet. Rosie gasped. Staring at her was a head with two eyes, a nose, and a mouth, and hair . . . hair that looked just like Mr. Quirk's. The head had no body and it was staring right at her.

5 · Something's Wrong!

Rosie hid in the corner, as far away from the head as she could get. Then she blinked hard and looked at it again. "It's not moving," she thought. Rosie crept a little closer to the head. "Mr. Quirk's wig! Daddy was right!" said Rosie out loud. The head was only a wooden wig stand, and on it was Mr. Quirk's wig.

"That's it!" she said. "The wig. I'll bring them the wig. The gang knows he has false teeth, but they don't know he has false hair. Besides, the gang may be wrong about his teeth. I'll bet he only has one set . . . and he's wearing it. And that's why I can't find any teeth." As she talked, her own teeth stopped chattering for the first time since she had begun sneaking around Mr. Quirk's apartment. "I'll take them the wig. It's even better than false teeth." Rosie grabbed the wig and climbed out the window. "Wait till the gang sees this!"

Quickly, she took off her disguise and stuffed everything into the shopping bag. Then she ran to the center of the park. She almost ran into Mrs. Samuels and her dog, Elmer, who were leaving the park.

"Too hot for us, Rosie my dear. Has that brother of yours been good to you?" asked Mrs. Samuels.

"Oh, yes," Rosie stammered.

"Well, that's nice to hear about George," said Mrs. Samuels. "I hope the boy keeps it up."

Rosie dashed over to the gang. "I did it. I did it!" Rosie was out of breath, but grinning. "Mr. Quirk doesn't only wear false teeth. He wears false . . ." and Rosie took out the wig and plopped it on George's head.

"Hair!" shouted the gang. "Hair!" And they all rolled over the grass, laughing as hard as they could.

George tossed the wig to Helen. "Disgusting!" he yelled.

Helen tossed the wig to Peter.

"Where are the teeth?" asked George. "Where are the teeth?"

"Oh, I couldn't find any," said Rosie proudly. "It's clear he only has one pair. Right huh, huh? Anyway, you dodo, how could I find his teeth if he's not there? When he's not there, he's wearing them, right? . . . right. . . ."

"Not right. We're sure he has more than one pair, at least a second pair," said George. "So he can grind his teeth and have a different mean look each time he gets mad at us."

"Well, he doesn't," said Rosie, "and that's that." But now Rosie was not sure at all.

Peter tossed the wig to Billy.

"Give it back to me, give it back," said
Rosie. "I have to take it back now . . .
before he comes home!"

Billy tossed her the wig, and Rosie ran as
fast as she could across the park, behind
their house, and through Mr. Quirk's back
window.

The gang could hardly believe it when
Rosie returned to the park so quickly. She
had made it just in time. As she sat down,
Rosie looked back at the house. Mr. Quirk
was walking through the front door of his

apartment. Rosie shuddered. Then she said quietly, "I did the dare. I did it. Now I can have my shrimp rules. Now you can show me the secret handshake." Rosie looked around at the gang. But no one was looking back at her, and no one was getting up to show her the secret handshake.

"Is something wrong? Did Mr. Quirk find out what I did?" Rosie asked. She could feel the *huh, huhs* again.

"Come on, George, tell her," said Lizzie, moving closer to Rosie.

"You tell her," said George.

"The gang decided you didn't do the dare right," said Lizzie.

"What?" said Rosie. "What do you mean, I didn't do the dare right?"

"Well," said George. "Well, remember I said you had to do everything just like we said?"

"Yeah, well," shouted Rosie, "well, I did do everything just like you said."

"Everything except one thing," said George.

"What one thing?" asked Rosie. "Huh, huh . . .?"

"You didn't get the teeth. You got the wig," said George.

"But that's not fair, not fair!" Rosie started to shout again. "I couldn't find any false teeth."

"The dare was to get at least one pair of his false teeth," said George. "That was the dare and you almost did it. But you didn't get the teeth. So you can't play baseball with the gang. And you won't be able to have your shrimp rules."

Rosie started to cry. "Maybe I didn't look hard enough," she thought to herself.

"Don't worry, Rosie," said Lizzie. "The gang is going to give you a second chance."

"Oh, no," said Rosie, her teeth beginning to chatter again. "I can't go in there again," she cried, pointing to Mr. Quirk's apartment. "I can't. It's too scary. I can't do it again."

"The new dare won't be so bad," said George. "And you won't have to do anything like go inside any dark places. You can do it right here in the park with all of us watching. Okay?"

Rosie didn't answer.

"Deal?" asked George.

"Wait a minute," said Rosie. "You're sure this dare's easier?"

"Yes," said George.

"Yes," agreed the gang.

"When will you tell me what the dare is?" asked Rosie.

"Right now," said George.

6 · The Second Dare

"Right now?" cried Rosie. "Right now?"

"Yes, right now," said George, looking over at Mrs. Samuels. The gang looked over at Mrs. Samuels, too.

"Look," said Norman, "everything's fine. She's taking one of her famous park-bench snoozes." Everyone started to laugh. Everyone, that is, except Rosie.

"What's so funny?" asked Rosie, twisting the ends of her ponytail again. "Why are you talking about Mrs. Samuels?"

"Shhh," said Helen. "This may be her most famous nap. I think I can hear her snoring from all the way over here."

The gang all stopped talking and listened.

"I can hear her, I can hear her," said Norman. "Record-breaking snoozing. She belongs in the *Guinness Book of World Records*."

"Sounds like a powerful buzz saw," giggled Helen.

"Like the world's loudest queen bee." Peter laughed. He bent down and held his arms out like wings. "Buzzz, buzzz, buzzz," he buzzed.

"Yeah," said Norman, holding his ears and laughing. "I'm going home to get my earplugs."

"Oh, cut it out!" shouted Rosie. "You guys are really mean. Mrs. Samuels is my friend. I bet some of you guys snore, too."

"Buzz, buzz, buzz," said Peter again.

That just made Rosie madder. "Mrs. Samuels gets tired," she said. "It's hard work taking care of Elmer, and she needs her beauty sleep. That's what my dad says.

45

You are being dispectful, real dispectful."

"You mean disrespectful," interrupted George.

"Dispectful, disrespectful, whatever," said Rosie. "Whatever it is, however you say it, don't be it. Huh, huh."

George looked over at Mrs. Samuels again. "She's still sleeping, so we don't have to worry. Everything's ready, if you are, Rosie," said George.

"I'm ready," said Rosie, pushing her bangs off her forehead. "So what's the dare? What's the dare? Yes, I am ready to get all this dare business over with." Rosie nodded her head yes. She didn't even feel any *huh, huhs* racing all over her body. In fact, she felt calm.

"This is the second dare, Rosie," said Norman. "The rules are the same as the first dare. You must do the dare exactly as we tell you and not tell anyone . . . ever . . . about it."

"I know all that," said Rosie. "Just tell me what it is."

Rosie looked down at her knees. This

time, they weren't even shaking.

"The dare is," said Norman, looking over at Mrs. Samuels. "The dare is to let Elmer off his leash while Mrs. Samuels is taking one of her queen-bee snoozes. And then when she wakes up and discovers Elmer is gone, tell her you let him off his leash because you wanted to prove to her that Elmer doesn't need to be tied up all the time."

"What!" yelled Rosie. Rosie wasn't scared this time. She was mad. "What?" Her voice was getting louder and louder. George started to cover his ears. "You're going to make me do something to Mrs. Samuels?" screamed Rosie. Now she could feel the *huh, huhs* again.

"George," she yelled, shaking her fist at him.

"*You* talk to her. *You* explain it, George," said Norman. "I can't deal with her."

George took his hands off his ears and looked at Rosie. "You want your shrimp rules, don't you, Rosie?"

Rosie stopped yelling.

"You see, Rosie, you are not doing anything to Mrs. Samuels. You are just doing
something to Elmer," explained George,
"not to—"

"No, I don't see," said Rosie. "Elmer is
Mrs. Samuels'—"

"Oh, Rosie, you dodo. Elmer is a dog, and
Mrs. Samuels is a—" said George.

"I know the difference between a dog and
a person," said Rosie.

"Well," said George, "you're not doing
something directly to Mrs. Samuels. I told
the gang you wouldn't do that."

"Oh, thanks," said Rosie sourly. "Oh,
thanks."

"Do you want to listen, Rosie, or not?"
said George.

"Okay," she said. "Go, on."

"Mrs. Samuels always blames me for
everything. So we thought the dare should
make Mrs. Samuels get mad at you for once
and see that I'm not the only kid who does
bad things, that you do bad things sometimes, too."

Rosie gave George a nasty look.

"And, Rosie," said George, "we figured that this dare would be good for Elmer. The gang really feels sorry for him. Mrs. Samuels never lets him off his leash when he's outside. Never. Elmer's probably never had a chance to run."

Rosie started twirling her ponytail, wishing they had made her cut off her hair instead. Rosie felt that doing something to Elmer was really like doing something to Mrs. Samuels.

"Well, Rosie? Deal?" asked George. "What's taking you so long?"

"Wait a minute, just one minute," she said.

"I'll just tell Mrs. Samuels," thought Rosie to herself, "that I figured Elmer would like a run and that I was watching him to make sure he didn't run off and that it was all my idea. But of course she'll really think it was George's idea, and. . . ." Rosie's mind raced on. "And she'll blame George just like she always does. And I'll get my shrimp rules from the gang." Rosie smiled.

"Deal," said Rosie, as she shook hands very hard with George. Then she shook hands with all the other members of the gang. "When I finish, you'll show me the secret handshake, too?"

"Yes," said George, "but you'd better do the dare now, before Mrs. Samuels wakes up."

Rosie crept over to the bench. Carefully, she took Elmer's collar off his leash. Elmer sat still, just like he always did. Rosie looked up at Mrs. Samuels. "She's still asleep and Elmer hasn't moved an inch. And when she wakes up, I'll have my shrimp rules."

Just as Rosie reached over to pat Elmer on the head, the dog made a dash to the bench on the other side of the park. Rosie couldn't believe Elmer was running so fast. But she was sure he'd come right back. Rosie looked over at the gang. They were all pointing at Elmer and laughing.

Rosie was getting nervous now. "Here, Elmer," she said in a soft voice, careful not

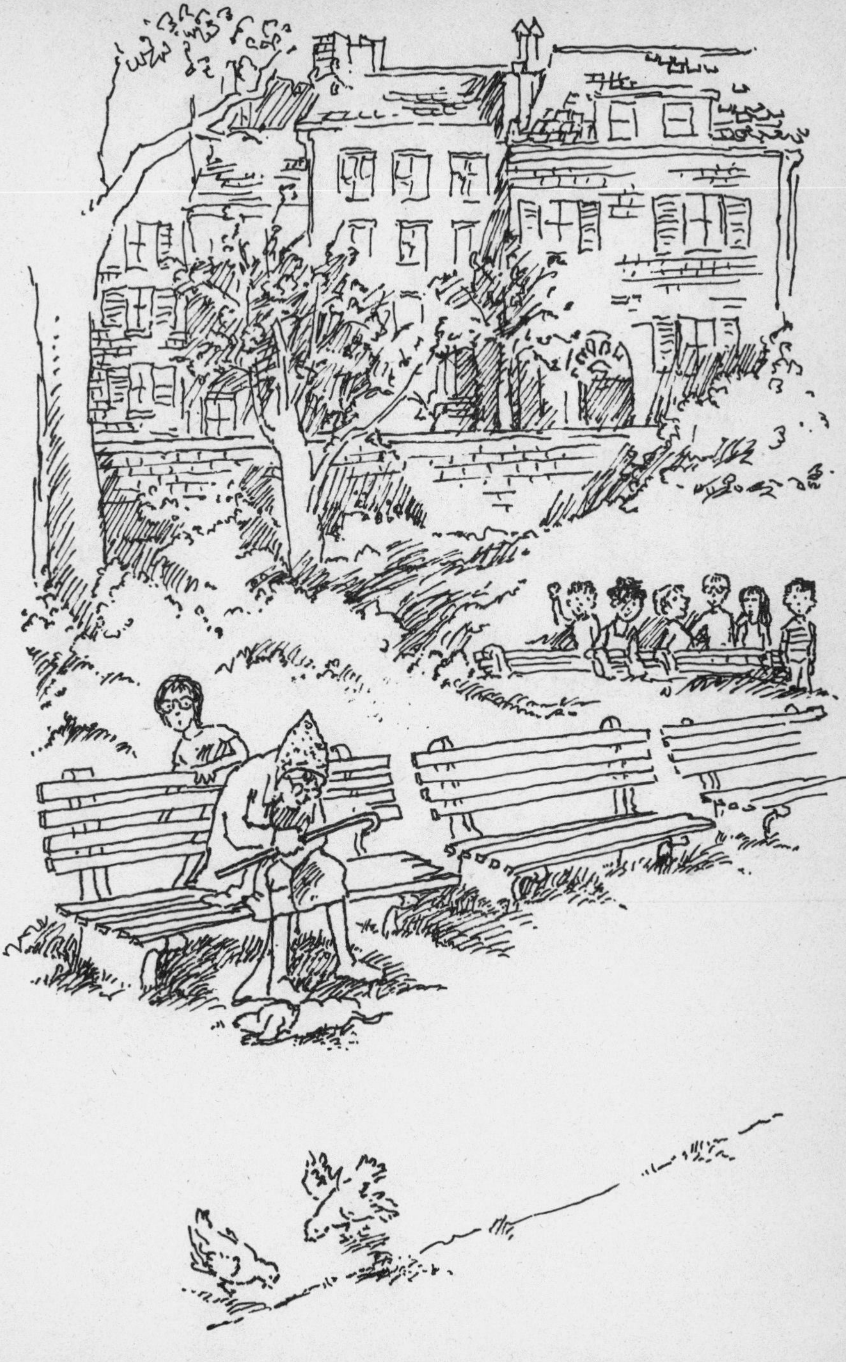

to wake Mrs. Samuels. Rosie was sure Elmer would come back to the bench, to Mrs. Samuels. After all, he had never, ever, left her side, never. As Rosie began walking over to him, it looked as if Elmer was going to obey her. But instead, he stretched his legs, and raced across the park—and right across Willard Street.

Rosie tied her new running shoes tight. Then she raced across the park and across Willard Street. She could still see Elmer running down Willard Street toward Rutland Square. Rosie ran as fast as she could, calling, "Elmer, Elmer! Come back!"

7 • The Storm

Rosie was running so hard and fast she almost ran right into Mr. Quirk, who was carrying a big brown box. "Slow down, Davidson child," he muttered, giving her a mean stare. Rosie thought she could even hear him grind his teeth. "Sorry," she said, trying to keep an eye on Elmer in the distance. But Elmer was getting farther away and looking smaller and smaller.

Elmer crossed Mt. Auburn Street. Rosie crossed Mt. Auburn Street. Now she was afraid of losing him in the crowd of shoppers. It was hard to keep her eye on the traffic light and the cars and buses and

Elmer, too. When the light changed, she crossed the street in the fastest walk she had ever walked. Her mother had always told her *never* to run across the street, always to walk.

Elmer was slowing down. He stopped to sniff an old candy wrapper. Now he was only half a block ahead of Rosie. But just as she reached Elmer, he dashed across the street, right in front of a woman on roller skates. The woman yelled at Rosie, "Keep your silly-looking mutt out of the street, kid. He almost wiped me out!"

"Sorry," said Rosie. Both her mother and her father had told her never, never to cross a street in the middle of the block. So Rosie knew that she shouldn't cross in the middle. But she also knew that if she went back to the corner, she would lose sight of Elmer. And then she'd never find him again.

Rosie took a deep breath, looked both ways, and did her fast street-cross walking. When she got to the other side, she spotted Elmer halfway up the block, running behind a very large Dalmatian. Rosie ran after them.

Elmer and the Dalmatian crossed another street. Rosie kept on running. Then, the Dalmatian turned and ran into an alley. Elmer turned and followed the Dalmatian into the alley.

Rosie looked up at the sky. Suddenly it had turned dark. Large gray and black storm clouds were moving fast across the sky, making shadows along the ground. Rosie began to shiver. All she had on were her new running shorts and a cotton T-shirt.

She looked down the alley where Elmer and the Dalmatian had run. It was dark and dreary. And she couldn't see Elmer or the Dalmatian any more. "I can't go in there. It's too scary and maybe it's even unsafe. Now I've really lost Elmer. All because of those stupid shrimp rules," she thought.

Rosie sat down on the steps of a store that was next to the alley. She looked up at the sign on the door. "Closed on Saturdays—for the summer," it said. Above it was a bigger sign that read "Heilbrun's Discount Woolens." Rosie had never seen this store before. In fact, she had never seen this whole block.

She had been so busy trying not to lose sight of Elmer and keeping an eye on cars as she crossed all the streets, that she hadn't noticed where she was going.

The sky was turning darker and the wind was starting to blow hard. "I'm lost," Rosie cried to herself. "I'm lost and I've lost Elmer."

Just then, lightning flashed across the sky. Then Rosie heard a big crash of thunder and she covered her ears. It began to pour. The rain came down so fast and so hard that it felt as if little stones were hitting her all over her body. Rosie shivered again. This time, she wasn't just shivering from fear. She was cold and wet and miserable.

Rosie huddled under the ragged awning of Heilbrun's Discount Woolens. "I don't have any money to call home. Even if I did, I can't call home, because I haven't caught Elmer yet. Maybe he'll just come back out of the alley. Oh, maybe if I cross my fingers and say 'Pretty please, pretty please, with butter and cheese!' he'll come out. And

56

anyway, I can't go home." Rosie could feel the *huh, huhs* again. "Mom and Dad will be so mad at me for going more than five blocks away from Willard Street on my own."

"Come, Elmer. Come, Elmer," shouted Rosie as she hugged herself trying to get warm. But Elmer didn't come out of the alley.

Rosie started to sob. "I'm lost, I'm lost, all because of George and this stupid dare business." Rosie couldn't stop crying. And she couldn't stop shivering.

8 · Foul Play

When the rain came, George and the gang ran from the park, up the steps to George's house.

"Oh, dear," said Mrs. Davidson when she opened the door. "Come in and get out of this miserable rain."

"Uh, we're having a meeting up in my room. We don't want to bother you, Mom," said George.

"Oh, you won't bother me. We're watching the ball game. But they just announced a rain delay. Too bad. The Red Sox and the Yankees are tied. Say, where's Rosie?"

58

"Uh," said George, "uh . . . well. . . ."

"Well, where is she?" asked his mother.

"Well," said George slowly, "you see, somehow Elmer got off his leash. Rosie went to look for him. He ran across the park and Rosie thought she'd better get him."

Norman looked out the door. He could see Mrs. Samuels running into her house. "Psst," he whispered to Lizzie. "Mrs. Samuels knows."

"What's that, Norman?" asked Mrs. Davidson.

"Oh, ah, oh . . ." Norman said, "I was just telling Lizzie to look at the rain. It sure is coming down. And all that lightning and thunder."

"Poor Rosie out in that storm," said Mrs. Davidson. "I hope she's keeping dry somewhere. . . ." Mrs. Davidson looked a little worried. So did George.

"Don't worry, Mom," George said. "She'll be back soon."

"I guess a little rain won't hurt her,"

sighed Mrs. Davidson. "If you kids want to watch the ball game, Dad and I are in the living room."

"We'll be up in my room, Mom. The gang's having a meeting," said George.

George and the gang ran up the stairs to George's room and slammed the door behind them. George turned on the radio.

"Turn it off, George," said Peter. "We have to figure out what to say to Mrs. Samuels. Then we can listen to the game."

George turned off the radio. He paced back and forth across the room. "Whatever happens, Mrs. Samuels will blame me for everything."

"So what if she blames you?" said Lizzie. "That's nothing new. Let's just hope she doesn't find out about the dare. Then the whole gang's in big trouble."

"What about Rosie?" said Helen. "What if she tells about the dare?"

"Give Rosie some credit," said Lizzie. "She's not a baby any more. And besides, if she tells about the dare, she won't get her shrimp rules. And Rosie wants to play baseball. So . . . she won't tell."

"Well, what are we going to do?" asked Helen.

"Nothing," George said. "Nothing. Rosie will be back soon, and everything will be all right. Everyone cool it. Cool it! Be cool."

George turned on the radio again. "The rain delay is over. It's the bottom of the sixth inning. The score is tied at four-all. The score, folks—"

"George," called Mrs. Davidson. "Telephone for you."

George ran into the hall and picked up the telephone.

"Maybe it's Rosie," said Lizzie.

"Maybe," Bill said, "it's Mrs. Samuels."

The gang stood around, waiting for George to get off the phone.

George raced back into the room.

"Who was it?" shouted Peter.

"It was Mattie," George said.

"Mattie?" yelled Lizzie. "What did *she* want?"

"If you'll all shut up, I'll tell you," said George. "Mattie and the Rutland Square Gang saw us playing ball yesterday. They challenged us to a game tomorrow—at twelve noon. The Rutland Square Gang against the Willard Street Gang."

"Did you say yes?" asked Helen.

"Of course. I told them we would smear them," said George. Then his voice lowered. "If we ever get out of this mess today . . . I wish I had never thought of shrimp rules and double dares."

Suddenly the doorbell rang.

"I'll get it!" shouted George. "I'll bet it's Rosie!" George and the gang raced down the stairs. George opened the front door. Standing at the door was Mrs. Samuels, holding an empty leash.

Mrs. Samuels walked right past George and into the living room, dragging Elmer's leash behind her.

"Foul play, foul play!" she screamed.

"Do come in and sit down," said Mrs.

Davidson. "I bet you don't mean foul play, but rather foul ball."

"No, no, no," said Mrs. Samuels, swinging Elmer's leash in the air, just missing the top of Mrs. Davidson's head. "I'm talking about Elmer. Elmer has disappeared. There's been some foul play here." She turned and looked at George. "Some foul play here," she said again.

"I can't imagine that the gang had anything to do with Elmer's running away," said Mr. Davidson. "He just got off the leash. And Rosie went to find him. You probably forgot to hook Elmer to the leash, or the clip was just worn out or. . . ."

"I was not careless with Elmer and never am," said Mrs. Samuels, beginning to cry. "Someone let him go."

Mr. Davidson got up and walked Mrs. Samuels over to the couch. "Look, we're all a little worried about Elmer and Rosie. But they'll be back soon. Let's watch the ball game. It will take our minds off them. After all, you are one of the Red Sox's biggest fans."

Mrs. Samuels sat down on the couch between Mr. and Mrs. Davidson. She wiped her eyes. "What's the score, George?" she asked. "You're the baseball expert."

George tried to answer, but the words wouldn't come out of his mouth. "Four to four," he said finally, in a scratchy voice.

"Speak up, child. I can hardly hear you," said Mrs. Samuels.

"Four to four," he shouted.

"I'm not deaf, young man," she said.

"I'm sorry, Mrs. Samuels," answered George in a lower voice. "I didn't mean to shout. I think I'll go out on my bike and look for Rosie."

"And Elmer, too?" asked Mrs. Samuels.

Mr. Davidson turned away from the television. "No, George, you are not going to look for Rosie or Elmer. I don't need two lost children."

"Three, if you count Elmer," said Mrs. Samuels.

"Now, everyone stop worrying. Rosie is almost nine years old. She knows the neighborhood well. She'll be back soon," said Mr. Davidson.

"She has been gone for over an hour," said Mrs. Davidson.

"Let's not panic," said Mr. Davidson. "If Rosie—"

"And Elmer," said Mrs. Samuels.

"And Elmer," sighed Mr. Davidson, "are not back in fifteen minutes, then I'll go out and look for them."

"Well," said Mrs. Samuels, looking at her watch, "if they're not back in fifteen minutes, I'm calling the police!"

George and the gang didn't say anything. They just kept staring at the television set.

9 • Fly Ball

"I wish I knew where I was," moaned Rosie, sitting on the steps of Heilbrun's Discount Woolens. The sun was peeking through the gray storm clouds now, and it made her squint. Her throat was dry. Her stomach felt empty. "If I start walking," she thought, "I can probably find my way home."

Rosie looked down the alley. It was full of big puddles. Now that the sun was out, she could see all the way through to the other side of the alley, but she didn't see Elmer anywhere. "I can't go home without Elmer," she said to herself. "I can't."

Rosie could see her reflection in the store window. "I look awful," she said out loud.

She twisted her ponytail, and water ran down her back. She shivered again.

Rosie took one last look in the window. Then she walked down the street toward the corner. The street sign said Boylston Street. "I've been on Boylston Street before," she thought, "but when was I here and where is it, exactly?"

She looked around for Elmer. "Now that the sun's out, maybe Elmer's come out, too," she thought. "Elmer! Elmer, you dodo, Elmer," she called.

Rosie passed a woman selling hot roasted peanuts. The warm smell made her search around in her pocket for some change. Then she remembered that she didn't have any money. Rosie looked at a clock at a gasoline station. "Four-thirty—it's almost dinner time." Then she passed a man selling hot dogs. She stood and stared at the man, hoping he would see how hungry she was and offer her one for free. Then she remembered her father's warning: "Never accept anything from a stranger."

Rosie kept on walking. She began to call,

"Elmer, Elmer," again. But this time her voice was very soft, almost a whisper.

She passed a policewoman. "Are you lost, little girl? Can I help you?" the policewoman asked Rosie.

"Oh, I'm fine," Rosie muttered.

"Well, if you need anything, I'll be right here on this corner," the policewoman called after her.

Rosie crossed the street. She stood in front of a huge building. It was red and green and looked to Rosie like a giant barn about six stories high. "Maybe they build giant airplanes or rockets in there," she thought. "George would like it here. I wish George was with me. Then we could explore the place. There are lots of police around here. Maybe it's a top-secret operation. Some secret launching could be going on here."

Rosie kept walking around the giant barn. She passed a big truck with cables and wires coming out of it. The side of the van had a big sign with red and white letters on it—"TV 48," read Rosie.

"TV 48," she thought. "Whatever's happening in there is important if TV 48 is here."

Suddenly Rosie heard a loud roar from inside the building. Then there was a lot of yelling and clapping. Rosie kept on walking. She heard another loud roar. Then she came to a big gate. "How dumb can I be?" she said to herself. "It's Fenway Park." On top of the gate a big sign read:

FENWAY PARK—HOME OF THE BOSTON RED SOX
TODAY'S GAME:
BOSTON RED SOX VS. THE NEW YORK YANKEES

"Oh, my goodness," Rosie said out loud. "I really am at Fenway Park!"

Rosie stopped walking and looked at the sign again. Then she remembered that it was Mrs. Samuels who had told her all about Fenway Park. She also remembered that Mrs. Samuels always brought Elmer to watch the Red Sox practice. And that the players always gave Elmer old baseballs to chew on.

"Elmer's got to be inside—looking for old balls. And I've got to get inside and find him," said Rosie.

Rosie looked down the street and saw the policewoman looking back at her. She knew she couldn't go in through the front gate. She didn't have a ticket, and she didn't have any money to buy one.

Rosie turned around, walked past the policewoman, past the front gate, past all the guards, past the people selling peanuts and hot dogs to the back of the stadium.

"Mrs. Samuels always says Fenway Park is like a second home to Elmer. He's got to be somewhere inside Fenway Park." Rosie heard another roar from the crowd. "I've got to find a door. Maybe there's a special door that the TV people with the cameras and cables use." Rosie walked back and tried the door next to the TV truck. It was locked shut in three places.

"Oh, I'll never get in. I'll never get in." Rosie shook her head. It was hopeless.

Rosie walked around to the other side of the stadium. She started to cry. A man selling balloons asked her if she wanted one. Rosie shook her head no and walked on. The crowd roared. Rosie wiped her eyes and looked over at the stadium. There, to her left, was a door halfway open. There was no sign on the door, and it was painted the same color as the stadium. Even the handle was painted green.

"This looks like a secret or private door," Rosie thought. "I bet when it's closed, you can't even tell there's a door here." Rosie looked up and down the street. She couldn't see the policewoman any more, and most of the people with carts were busy selling.

Rosie pushed the door all the way open. Everything inside looked dark and smelled like sweaty old sneakers.

Rosie started to shiver again. Then she thought, "If I could go into Mr. Quirk's, I can go in here. Besides, this is my only chance to get Elmer, the only way to get in, so I've got to go in, huh, huh. I've got to go in."

Rosie put one foot inside the door. The opening was too tight for her to fit through.

She opened the door a little more. It creaked. Rosie jumped back. Then she realized the noise was just a rusty hinge. She stepped inside the door and closed it behind her. It creaked shut.

It was so dark Rosie could hardly see, but she could hear something. As her eyes became used to the darkness after the bright sunshine, Rosie saw a dim light hanging from the ceiling. The light was swinging back and forth, making shadows on the wall, as if someone had given it a push.

Rosie tried to tell herself to calm down. She felt that if she could just calm down, she would be able to find another door that led out to the playing field. Then Rosie thought she saw an opening that might be a door. She tiptoed toward it. She saw something that made her jump back in horror. She could make out a shape on the floor in the darkness. And it was breathing.

As Rosie jumped backwards, she bumped into a bench and flipped over, landing on top of a pile of wet towels.

"It sure is smelly here," she thought as she landed. "Yuk!"

She stood up and looked over at the breathing noise. It hadn't moved.

Rosie tiptoed toward the opening again. Just as she passed the breathing noise, it rolled over, stood up and grabbed her untied shoelace with its teeth.

"Let go!" screamed Rosie. She yanked back her foot as hard as she could. The noise let go and growled. Then it yowled.

"Oh, Elmer. It's you, Elmer. I'd know that yowl anywhere. You're the breathing noise. Oh, Elmer, I've found you," cried Rosie.

As Rosie bent down to pick up Elmer, he raced through the opening and into a long tunnel. Rosie ran after him. The tunnel was

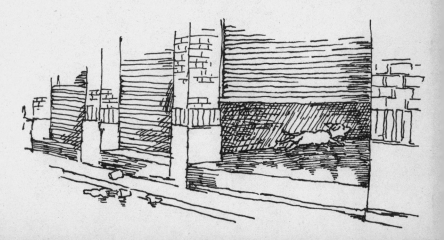

long and dark and musty smelling. But suddenly Rosie could see light at the other end and she could hear the crowd roar. Elmer raced out the other end of the tunnel. Rosie's heart was racing, too. "I've got to capture Elmer," she said to herself. "I almost had him. I scared him in the dark. He didn't know me. Poor Elmer, cold and wet and lost, just like me."

Rosie raced to the end of the tunnel. "I'll get him this time, I'll get him." Rosie raced right out on the field. She ran over home

plate. Then she ran over the pitcher's mound. She knew she had to keep an eye on Elmer this time or she would never catch him. She kept on running after Elmer. She could hear people in the grandstands screaming, "Stop the game." But Rosie kept on running.

Elmer was deep into right field by then. Just as Rosie reached him, Elmer jumped high in the air and caught a fly ball in his mouth. Rosie tried to tackle Elmer. But she missed and crashed right into the Red Sox's

all-star right fielder. "Sorry," she said as she
lunged after Elmer. Finally, Rosie caught
Elmer by the collar. But Rosie and Elmer
and the right fielder crashed into each other
again. They all slid into a giant mud puddle
left from the thunderstorm. Rosie held onto
Elmer as tight as she could, not daring to
look up. All she could hear were voices—
angry, puzzled voices.

"What are you doing here?" asked one
voice.

"This is an official game. There are laws
against this," another voice said.

"Who's the mutt?" a third voice demanded.

"She's ruined the game," said the first voice. "Get the kid off the field."

"Is this some kind of a joke or something?" said the third voice.

By this time, the whole Red Sox team had left the dugout and circled around Rosie and Elmer.

"That mutt looks familiar to me," said Chi-Chi Clem, the Red Sox manager. "I know . . . that's Elmer. It's Elmer. Mrs. Samuels' dear, darling Elmer. But who's the kid?"

Rosie held on to Elmer with all her might.

"Now I'm in trouble," she thought. "Big League trouble."

10 • Real Live TV

George and the gang moved closer to the television set.

"There seems to be some commotion on the field," said the television reporter.

"Not another delay," moaned Mr. Davidson.

"There will be a slight delay," said the sports reporter. "It looks like some eager fan just ran out on the field. We are sending our crew down to the field to get a first-hand report. Bear with us, folks. This may cause problems in a four-to-four tie game."

"I wish we could see," said Lizzie.

"Folks, stay with us," said the reporter.

"We still haven't got the full story. It's hard to tell from up here in the press box. The fan seems to be surrounded by the team and the umpires. We just now see that the head of the Baseball Association is being driven in the Red Sox car over to the action. Folks, this must be something serious. I have been broadcasting the Red Sox for over twenty years, yes, folks, for over twenty years. . . ."

"I wish this idiot would stop blithering and tell us what's going on," said Mrs. Samuels. "I've had the unhappy experience of having to listen to him for over twenty years."

"Well," said the TV reporter, "we're still setting up our cameras, but it looks like some little kid lost her dog and ran out on the field."

"Oh, no," moaned George. "What if it's Ro—"

"You be quiet now," said Mrs. Samuels. "I can't hear a thing that blithering idiot is saying."

"Folks, I now turn you over to our camera

crew on the field," said the reporter. "At this very minute they're talking with players and coaches on the spot. Come in, Gingie, and tell the folks at home the full story. Are you with me?"

"Yes, I'm with you. This is Gingie Polk from WWIN–TV. Channel 48, your all-sports station. Tune us in for every sports event. We are there for you, folks, our fans."

"Another blithering idiot," said Mrs. Samuels.

"You're not kidding," said Norman.

Just then, Mrs. Samuels jumped right out of her seat and ran up to the television set. "There they are!" she screamed.

"Who?" shouted Helen.

"Excuse me," said George in a very polite voice, "but if you could move please, Mrs. Samuels, and stop screaming, we could all see and hear what's happening."

Everyone quieted down.

"Yes, folks, this is Gingie Polk again. Now we finally have a view. It seems as if a little girl lost her dog. Wait a minute, folks.

Here's the Red Sox manager, Chi-Chi Clem. Chi-Chi, this is Gingie, WWIN–TV. Can you tell the folks what the situation is?"

Chi-Chi stuffed some chewing tobacco into the side of his cheek. "Well, we're trying to find out all the details. I know the mutt—name's Elmer—but I've never seen the kid before."

"I'll talk," said the right fielder. "I have plenty to say. The kid and the mutt ruined my play. Just when I was about to make the play that would have won us the game, the stupid dog ran by, jumped in front of me, and caught the fly ball. I'd have gotten it if

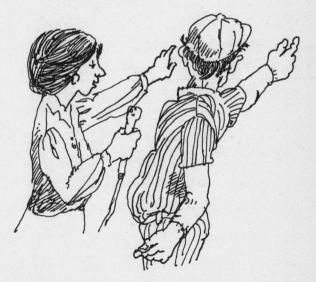

that little kid hadn't come running by and pushed me in the mud."

"Calm down, calm down," said Chi-Chi. "The umpire tells me there's nothing in the rule book about mutt interference, I mean, a dog getting in the way, so the umpires are trying to figure out what to do."

"Yes, folks, as you can see, there are some upset folks on this team," Gingie said. "And this is what makes for an exciting game, folks. Now if I can get myself through these players, I think the cameras can focus in on the little girl, and maybe we can find out why she's here, her story in her own words."

"Oh, no," cried George, looking over at the rest of the gang. "Now, we're done for."

"Folks, the camera is on the girl and the mutt. If I can get a little closer, I think we can get her to talk. Yes, folks, she will talk with me."

Rosie stood up, still holding Elmer in her arms. She straightened her glasses.

"What's your name?" Gingie asked.

"Rosie," said Rosie in a soft voice.

"Could you speak up into the microphone. You're on TV, channel 48 you know, WWIN," said Gingie Polk.

"Oh," Rosie said, "TV! Real, live TV?" She stood up very straight and grinned. "Hi there, all you sports lovers out there in TV Never-never-land. I'm Rosie and this is Elmer. Hi Mommy, hi Daddy, hi George, hi Mrs. Samuels, Elmer's fine, and hi there gang. I hope you're all watching. I'm on TV, huh, huh, real live TV." Rosie put her hand on her hip and almost dropped Elmer.

"Ahem," said Gingie Polk, "Rosie, now that you've introduced yourself, will you please tell the TV audience and all our fans your story, how you got here and why you got here?"

"Oh, sure," said Rosie, grabbing the mike. "Could you please hold Elmer for me? I don't want to lose him again."

The fans were silent. So were all the Red Sox players and so were the umpires and the coaches.

Rosie spoke into the microphone. "You see, I'm a really good baseball player myself. Well, not as good as you guys." Rosie looked over at the Red Sox players. "You see," she went on, "my brother George, he's two and a half years older than me. I'm almost nine . . . well, . . ." Rosie stopped talking.

"Is something wrong?" asked Gingie Polk.

"Noooo," said Rosie, who knew all of a sudden that she had to do some fast thinking.

"Then tell us what made you come here," said Gingie Polk.

"Uh," said Rosie, "well, here I am in Fenway Park. You're right, I am here. . . . You see, I had to catch Elmer."

"Can you please tell us why you had to catch Elmer?" asked Gingie Polk.

"I can't tell," said Rosie.

"What?" said Gingie Polk. "You can't tell!" Gingie Polk sounded amazed.

"I can't tell, huh, huh," said Rosie, trying to keep calm. "I won't tell . . . I promised my brother George I wouldn't tell."

"Rosie, you are on TV. The fans would really like the whole story," said Gingie Polk.

"Well," said Rosie, "ah, ah, I just knew Elmer was here. You see, Mrs. Samuels, my friend, and Elmer, her dog, have been coming to watch every baseball practice for nine years. And that man Chi-Chi . . ." Rosie pointed to the manager, "always gives Elmer old balls to chew on. Old balls are Elmer's favorite. I just *had* to get Elmer for Mrs. Samuels." Then Rosie started to cry. "I'm sorry I ruined the game!" she sobbed. "I just wanted to get Elmer back."

Chi-Chi rushed over, picked up Rosie, and gave her a hug. "You did a good thing for Mrs. Samuels—saving Elmer. Come on, Rosie," said Chi-Chi. "We're going to take the play over. You and Elmer come to the dugout, so we can cheer our team to victory." Chi-Chi picked up Elmer, too, and carried them over to the Red Sox dugout.

The television cameras followed closely.

"This is Gingie Polk, WWIN–TV, folks, with the story of the kid and the mutt. Now, back to baseball."

11 · Grounded

Lizzie leaned over to George and whispered in his ear. "Well, at least she didn't tell about the dare," said Lizzie.

"I know," sighed George. "I thought for sure the shrimp was going to spill the beans."

"She gets her shrimp rules now," said Norman. "She earned them."

"I know," moaned George. "I know." Still, George was worried. Rosie had said something about him on TV. Suddenly, George could feel that Mrs. Samuels was staring at him and the gang.

"George," said Mrs. Samuels, swinging

Elmer's leash in the air. "How could you do such a thing?"

George couldn't answer.

"You shouldn't blame George," said Mrs. Davidson. "After all, it wasn't his idea that Rosie go after Elmer."

"We'd better get over to Fenway Park and pick up Rosie," said Mr. Davidson.

"And Elmer," added Mrs. Samuels.

"You and the gang stay put until we return with the kid and the mutt." Mr. Davidson grinned.

George tried to grin back at his father, but a grin wouldn't form on his lips.

When Rosie arrived home, the whole gang, except for George, rushed over to greet her.

Lizzie gave her a big hug. "You were great," she said.

"I know," said Rosie.

"And you didn't spill the beans," added Norman, stealing a glance at Mrs. Samuels, who was holding Elmer tightly. Now Elmer was taking a nap.

"I know," said Rosie.

"And now you'll get your shrimp rules," said Peter.

"I know," said Rosie. She looked over at George, who was looking through his baseball fact book again.

"And—" said Bill.

"George," shouted Rosie. "George, George, did you see me on TV?"

George didn't answer.

"Did you seeee meee?" asked Rosie, with a giant grin on her face.

George still didn't answer.

"George?" said Rosie. "Geor—"

"Yes, I saw you," said George. "And I heard you tell about *me* on TV."

"But I didn't tell about the dare," whispered Rosie, "did I?"

"Big deal," said George.

"Were you ever on TV, huh, huh? Were you ever on TV with Gingie Polk of WWIN–TV?" Rosie sounded just like Gingie Polk.

Lizzie started to giggle.

Rosie walked over to George. She straightened her glasses and pointed her finger at him. "And did you ever sit on Chi-Chi Clem's lap?"

"Who would want to anyway?" said George.

"And," said Rosie, her voice getting higher and higher, "and," she yelled, pulling an autographed baseball out of her pocket, "what do you think of this, huh, huh? What do you think of this?"

"Who cares?" said George quietly. "Who cares?"

"What's that?" said Norman as he jumped up to look at the ball.

"A baseball with autographs of the whole Red Sox team, even Chi-Chi's," declared Rosie.

The whole gang examined the baseball.

"Excellent," said Helen, "excellent."

"We were glad to know you weren't lost," said Peter.

"Even George was glad you weren't lost," said Bill, looking over at George, who was reading his baseball fact book again. "At least, I think he was glad."

"Were you glad, George? Aren't you glad I'm safe?" said Rosie.

"Yes," mumbled George finally. "Yes, Rosie."

"And do you know what else?" asked Rosie. "Chi-Chi told me another good joke. Wanna hear it, wanna hear it?"

"Oh, no," sighed George, "another dumb joke."

"Your sister has excellent jokes," said Mrs. Samuels. "Go ahead, Rosie."

"Why are a cake and a baseball game alike?" asked Rosie.

"Cause they both need batters!" shouted George.

"You told the joke, you told the joke!" shouted Rosie. "That's not fair."

"Rosie, stop shouting," shouted Mrs. Davidson. "Daddy and I have something much more important to talk to you about." Rosie stopped shouting and looked at her parents. She knew what was coming.

"Rosie," said her mother. "Even though you did a good deed by finding Elmer, you did not obey your father and me."

"I didn't?" said Rosie, who knew she didn't.

"Yes," said her mother. "You went more

than five blocks from Willard Street on your own."

"But," said Rosie, "I had to get Elmer. George and the—"

"George didn't make you go, did he?" asked Mr. Davidson.

"Well, no, well, not exactly," said Rosie. George glared at Rosie. "Well, no, huh, huh," said Rosie, "no!"

"Then you are responsible for what you did, not George," said Mr. Davidson. "You are grounded for one week."

"What does that mean?" asked Rosie sadly.

"That means," said Mrs. Davidson, "you cannot play with the gang for one full week."

"But what about the challenge?" said Lizzie.

"What challenge?" asked Rosie.

"The Rutland Square Gang. Mattie's gang," Lizzie replied. "They challenged us to a baseball game tomorrow at twelve noon. And we *all* have to play in it, if we're going to have any chance of winning."

"The gang decided," said Norman.

"Decided what?" asked Rosie.

"We think you should play in the challenge game against the Rutland Square Gang," Norman went on. "Even if you can't hit."

"With my shrimp rules?" asked Rosie.

"Rosie will not be playing tomorrow, and that's that!" said Mr. Davidson. "I hope you all have that straight. You'll just have to play without her."

"But Norman's foot still hurts," moaned Lizzie. "We have to have Rosie play. She's a fast runner."

"No game for Rosie," said Mrs. Davidson.

"The Willard Street Gang can't turn down the challenge," moaned Rosie. "You guys better play without me. Hey, George, what about the secret handshake?"

"I'll show you tomorrow," said George.

The gang got their things and went out the front door. George started up the stairs. Rosie followed behind. Only Mr. and Mrs. Davidson and Mrs. Samuels were left in the living room.

George was glad Rosie was safe. And he did feel proud that she had not told about the dare—even though she probably blamed him for the whole mess. Still, he was sort of glad that she wasn't going to play against the Rutland Square Gang. After all, she still hit like a shrimp.

Then he thought again about Rosie getting lost. And he wondered if it was his fault, a little bit maybe. "If she hadn't been such a shrimp, none of this mess would have ever happened," he finally told himself. Still, George felt very mixed up. He wiped his head. He was hot and sweaty and very tired.

Rosie raced up the stairs past him. When she reached the door to her room, she turned to him and stuck out her tongue. Then she slammed the door behind her.

George slammed his door, too.

Even though George and Rosie were both in their rooms and both their doors were closed, they could still hear Mr. and Mrs. Davidson and Mrs. Samuels arguing. But neither George nor Rosie could hear what the three of them were arguing about.

12 · Another Shrimp

The next morning, Rosie felt a hand gently rubbing her shoulder. She stretched her arms out as far as she could reach and yawned. Then she curled back into a little ball.

"Rosie," said her father softly. "Rosie, wake up. I want to talk to you."

Rosie rubbed her eyes. "What?" she mumbled.

"Rosie," said her father, smiling, "I have good news for you. Well, at least some good news for you. You can play in the challenge today against the Rutland Square Gang."

"I can?" shouted Rosie. "You're kidding!"

She looked as if her eyes would pop out of her head.

"No, I'm not kidding. You are still grounded for the rest of the week. Mommy and I are still very upset with you about yesterday."

"What made you change your minds?" asked Rosie.

"An argument," said Mr. Davidson.

"With Mommy?" asked Rosie.

"With Mrs. Samuels," answered her father.

"That's what you guys were arguing about last night?" asked Rosie.

"Yep," said her father. "Mrs. Samuels said you should be able to play in the challenge today. After all you've been through, she said you deserved to play." Mr. Davidson smiled.

"She's right that I should play," yawned Rosie. "I am excellent." Then Rosie sat straight up in bed. "Does George know yet? Did George say he'll get me my shrimp rules for the big game today?"

"Yes," said Mr. Davidson. "I told George, and he said he'd do his best."

"He did!" shouted Rosie, jumping happily out of bed.

As George was getting dressed, he could hear Rosie screaming with delight. "I got my shrimp rules. George is the best brother in the whole wide world. I got my shrimp rules. And soon, I'll know the secret handshake."

"I guess I am the best brother in the whole wide world," said George to himself. Then he covered his ears with both hands. "There you go again," he yelled loud enough for Rosie to hear. "Screaming and yelling just like a shrimp."

It was eleven forty-five when the Rutland Square Gang lined up opposite the Willard Street Gang. As usual, Mrs. Samuels and Elmer were sitting on the park bench.

"Are we still agreed on the rules? Nine innings? Whoever wins is the neighborhood champ?" asked Mattie.

"Yes, Mattie," said George. "But,

but . . . we have one small addition to the rules."

Rosie started twisting her ponytail.

"Well, what is it?" said Mattie.

"It's about one of the littler kids on our team," said George. "She plays with some special rules—called shrimp rules and. . . ."

"You mean Rosie? I saw her on TV," said Mattie, grinning at Rosie. "I'm a Red Sox fan, too. I even have Chi-Chi Clem's autograph. But look, George, we agreed to the rules over the phone. And you agreed to no changes. So, no deal. No shrimp rules. You get it? No shrimp rules. Let's play."

"I want shrimp rules, too, for me," whined a voice from behind Mattie. It was one of the little kids from the Rutland Square Gang.

"How old are you, kid?" asked Rosie. "And what's your name?"

"My name's Lester, and I'm almost eight years old," said the kid. "They only let me play when somebody gets sick. It's not fair."

"I got it!" said Rosie. "Wouldn't it be fair if

both Lester and I got shrimp rules? One kid—"

"One shrimp—" muttered George, thinking one shrimp was enough for any game.

"One kid on each team would have shrimp rules. That would be even. That would be fair. Wouldn't it, wouldn't it, huh, huh?" said Rosie, her voice getting higher and higher.

"Cut out those *who-who-huh-huhs* so I can think," said Mattie.

Mattie paced back and forth. Rosie crossed her fingers and held her breath.

"Well, it's okay by me," said Mattie. "What about you, George?"

George didn't answer. Everyone stared at him, even Mrs. Samuels. Rosie held her breath. George *had* agreed to shrimp rules, but he could always change his mind and spoil everything.

"Okay," said George. "They can *both* have their shrimp rules."

Rosie ran over and gave George a big hug.

"Quit hugging me," said George, pushing Rosie away. "Let's get this game started."

Mrs. Samuels fished in her bag for a coin. Just as she stood up for the toss, Mr. Quirk walked over and sat down on the bench. Rosie tried not to look at him, but she couldn't help it. She took a quick look to see if he was wearing his wig. He glared back at her.

Rosie wondered if he had seen her on TV. Rosie wondered if he knew what she had done. Rosie felt shivers go up and down her spine. She hoped he wouldn't show his teeth today.

"Are you ready for the toss?" asked Mrs. Samuels.

George and Mattie shook hands. "We're ready," yelled both gangs. Elmer yowled.

"Heads or tails?" asked Mrs. Samuels.

"Tails," shouted Mattie.

"Heads," shouted George.

"Whoever wins the toss gets last ups," said Mrs. Samuels, "or as they said in my day, 'last licks' at bat!" She stood up, tossed the quarter in the air, caught it with one hand and plopped it on top of the other. She slowly lifted up her top hand. "Heads," she shouted. "Heads. Willard Street Gang has last licks."

"Not fair," whined Lester. "Not fair. . . ."

"Oh, no," moaned George. "Another shrimp whiner."

"Stop whining, Lester," said Rosie. "At least we got our shrimp rules."

104

13 · The Game

Lester was last up to bat for his gang. George pitched him grounders. He struck out.

Rosie was last up at bat for her gang. Mattie pitched her grounders. She struck out. In fact, Lester and Rosie struck out or were thrown out every time they came to bat.

By the bottom of the ninth inning, the score was eight to eight. And Mrs. Samuels and Elmer were snoozing on the park bench. Mattie was pitching and Bill had just struck out. He handed the bat to Rosie. Rosie took a couple of practice swings.

"Just lingering up," said Rosie.

"You mean, limbering up, don't you, Rosie?" said George. Rosie stuck out her tongue at him.

Rosie bent over, and stuck her fanny way out in back.

"Hey, Rosie, this isn't TV, you know," teased George.

"You never know when you're gonna be on real live TV, do you George?" trilled Rosie. "At least, I don't. . . ."

"Rosie, cut out the TV stuff. You've struck out or been thrown out every time," moaned George. "Just get *one* hit."

"I will get a hit this time," said Rosie. "I've been waiting until we really needed it. I've been saving up my power for now."

George shook his head.

All the players on the Willard Street Gang had their fingers crossed and their eyes on Rosie.

Rosie gripped her bat with all her might. Mattie rolled her a grounder. Rosie swung. She slammed the ball. It rolled up the first-base line. Then the ball rolled out of bounds, inches before first base.

"Oh, no!" cried Lizzie.

"Stt-rike one," shouted Lester.

"Oh, be quiet, you, you shrimp!" shouted Rosie.

Rosie took her TV stance again. Mattie rolled her another grounder. Rosie swung, and her bat hit the plate. She dropped the bat and ran to first base.

"Rosie," said Lester. "You never hit the ball. Your bat hit the plate."

Rosie straightened her glasses. She looked back at home plate. The ball was sitting on the plate. And the Rutland Square Gang was starting to boo.

Rosie walked back to home plate and picked up the bat again. She took her TV stance again. She straightened her glasses again. She gripped her bat again. Mattie rolled her a grounder again. Then Rosie whacked the ball as hard as she could. It flew between Mattie's legs and on out past Lester, who was playing short-stop.

Rosie ran and tagged first base. Then she kept on running and slid into second. Lester threw the ball to second, but not in time. Rosie was safe.

The whole Willard Street Gang cheered. They jumped up and down and hugged each other. Even George cheered. The cheering woke up Elmer and Mrs. Samuels. Mr. Quirk got up from the bench and walked out of the park, covering his ears.

Peter was up at bat next.

"The winning run is on second base," said George to Norman. "Sock it to them."

Peter struck out. Now it was George's turn. George picked up the bat and walked to the plate.

"You can do it, George," shouted Rosie. "Hit me home and the Willard Street Gang will beat the Rutland Square Gang. Hit me home!"

"Rosie, quit blithering, quit blabbering and pay attention to getting home," shouted Mrs. Samuels.

"Thank you, Mrs. Samuels," said George, and he tipped his Red Sox hat to her.

George took a couple of practice swings. Then he stood ready for Mattie's pitch. George hit the first ball hard out to left field. He ran as fast as he could, tagged first base, and then ran on to second.

As Rosie rounded third base, Lester scooped up the ball and ran toward her.

Mattie screamed, "Lester, you shrimp! Throw the ball home!" Lester threw the ball with all his might. The ball soared a good twenty feet past home plate.

"I scored the winning run!" shouted Rosie, as she tagged home plate. "I did it! I won the game for the Willard Street Gang!"

Then George tagged home plate with a big smile on his face.

"We won, we won!" shouted Mrs. Samuels from her bench.

"You won," said Mattie as she shook George's hand. "You won fair and square . . . even with shrimps playing."

"I'm not a shrimp," whined Lester.

"Me neither," whined Rosie.

"You won, even with a shrimp," said Mattie, patting Rosie on the back.

"In fact," said Rosie, "my shrimp rules won the game."

"No way," said George. "In fact, my hit won the game. It got you home."

"Hey, George, listen," said Rosie. "Please listen. Wanna hear the joke Lester told me?"

George covered his ears with his hands. "Noooo," he moaned.

"Please," moaned Rosie.

"Oh, okay, but this had better be a good one," said George.

"When is a baseball player," asked Rosie, "like a thief?"

"Don't know this one," said George, pretending he'd never heard it before.

"When he steals a base," said Rosie, starting to giggle.

"That's the dumbest joke I ever heard," said George, looking first at Rosie and then at Lester. "That must be a shrimp joke, 'cause shrimp jokes are dumb jokes."

"That was not a dumb joke," screeched Rosie.

George grabbed his mitt and baseball fact

book and ran toward his house. Rosie ran after him screaming, "That was not a dumb joke, huh, huh, that was not a shrimp joke. . . . And what about the secret handshake? You didn't show me the secret handshake. Not fair!"

"I dare you to make me," yelled George. "I double dare you!"

"It's a deal!" shouted Rosie.

And they ran across the park, yelling at each other all the way.

About the Author

ROBIE H. HARRIS received a masters degree at the Bank Street College and taught there for several years. Her expertise in the area of child development resulted in *Before You Were Three*. Her first book for younger children was *Don't Forget To Come Back* (Knopf), "Parents as well as children would benefit by her message." (Publishers Weekly)

Robie Harris lives in Cambridge, Massachusetts, with her husband Bill and their two sons, David who's eight and Ben who's ten.